GROWING THINGS

Angela Wilkes
Illustrated by John Shackell

CONTENTS

With thanks to Roger Priddy

W9-BXH-465

How plants grow

IT IS QUITE EASY TO GROW THINGS. BUT FIRST YOU HAVE TO UNDERSTAND WHAT MAKES PLANTS GROW AND GIVE THEM WHAT THEY NEED

Watching things grow

Roll about six sheets of paper towels into a tube and slide it into a big glass jar. Push different kinds of beans down between the jar and the paper. Wet the paper, then pour some water into the jar to keep the paper wet.

A PLANT CANNOT LIVE ON WATER ALONE. IF YOU WANT YOUR BEAN PLANTS TO GROW BIG, PUT THEM IN POTS WHEN THEY ARE ABOUT 6 in. TALL. *(See page 18)*

Put the jar in a warm place and look at it every day. The water will make the beans swell and split, then they will sprout. Watch what happens to the roots and shoots.

Things plants need

Plants need light for them to grow and make green leaves.

ALL PLANTS NEED WATER, BUT TOO MUCH WATER IS AS BAD FOR THEM AS TOO LITTLE. THEY LIKE RAINWATER BETTER THAN TAP WATER

YOU CAN BUY LIQUID PLANT FOOD. YOU ADD IT TO WATER AND POUR IT ON THE SOIL TO REPLACE THE FOOD THE PLANT HAS USED UP

Plants get their food and water from the soil. Their roots grow best in light, crumbly soil with a little peat and sand.

Potting soil for house plants is light soil with rich plant food in it.

Pots have holes in the bottom so water can drain out. If the soil gets soggy the roots of the plant will rot and die.

REMEMBER THAT PLANTS ARE LIVING THINGS. LOOK AFTER THEM CAREFULLY AND THEY WILL GROW STRONG AND HEALTHY

Gravel or bits of broken pot over the holes in the pots stop them from getting blocked, so that water can drain out of them easily.

A saucer under the pot catches the water.

3

Sowing seeds

Potting soil

seeds

watering can

seed tray

IF YOU PLANT SEEDS INDOORS IN SPRING THE SEEDLINGS WILL BE BIG ENOUGH TO PLANT OUTSIDE WHEN THE WEATHER IS WARM ENOUGH

sunflowers *zinnia* *nasturtiums*

An annual grows from seed, flowers and dies in one year.

foxgloves *pansies* *sweet william*

A biennial lives for two years. You plant it one year and it usually flowers the second year.

irises *geranium* *fuchsia* *paeonies*

A perennial lives and flowers for many years. It usually dies down in the winter, but grows again the next spring.

Fill a seed tray with potting soil. Sprinkle the seeds over it, then cover them lightly with more soil.

Water the seeds gently, using a watering can with a fine spray.

Tie a plastic bag over the tray and put it in a warm, dark place. The bag helps keep the soil damp.

DON'T PUT THE PLANTS IN DIRECT SUNLIGHT AS THEY WILL SHRIVEL. WATER THEM REGULARLY. THE SOIL SHOULD BE DAMP BUT NOT TOO WET

As soon as shoots appear, take the box out of the bag and put it in a warm, light place.

When the plants have six leaves, replant them 2in. apart in new trays, so they have more room to grow.

GREEDY GRUB

WATCH OUT FOR GREEDY GRUBS

As soon as the weather is warm enough, move the trays outside, so the plants get used to being outdoors.

When they have grown too big for the trays, dig them up very carefully, keeping the soil around their roots.

Dig small holes in the garden and carefully plant the seedlings in them. Press the soil down around them, then water them.

5

Sunflowers

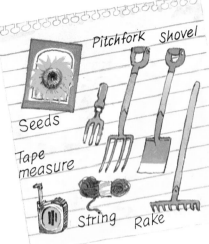

Seeds
Pitchfork
Shovel
Tape measure
String
Rake

Giant sunflowers grow very fast. You can plant the seeds outside.

Plant the seeds in the spring. Choose a sunny place with good soil, near a fence or a wall if possible.

Pull up all the weeds, then dig and rake the ground, so the soil is level and does not have any lumps in it.

Water the ground every day and shoots will appear in 10-14 days. The plants will grow very fast if you remember to water them. You could have a race with a friend to see whose sunflower grows the fastest (or tallest).

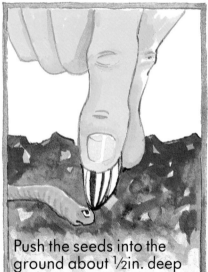

Push the seeds into the ground about ½in. deep and 24in. apart, so they have room to grow.

TIE THE SUNFLOWER TO A STICK AS IT GROWS, TO STOP IT FROM FLOPPING OVER

Sunflowers grow 9-13 feet tall. Measure them every week. They flower from July to September.

The flowers are the size of dinner plates and turn around to face the sun. Bees love them.

When the flowers die, cut off one of the heads and rub the seeds out onto some newspaper with a fork.

Put the seeds in an envelope. Seal it and label it, then keep it in a dry place and plant the seeds next year.

7

Growing trees

Pots and saucers

Potting soil

Pebbles

Pitchfork

Plastic bags

Plant a tree. In ten years it will be a home for many birds and insects, and it may live to be hundreds of years old.

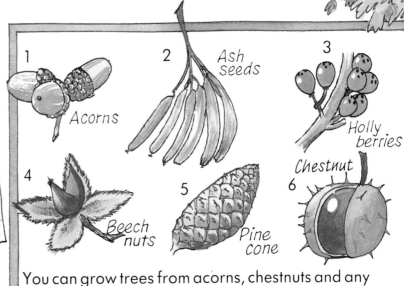

1 Acorns

2 Ash seeds

3 Holly berries

4 Beech nuts

5 Pine cone

6 Chestnut

You can grow trees from acorns, chestnuts and any other tree seeds you find in autumn. Keep a note of what you find, so you know which seedling is what later on. You can also collect fruit seeds to plant.

Plastic bag

Saucer

Plant each seed in a small pot. Water it, then tie a plastic bag over the pot. This keeps the soil damp.

Put the pots on a windowsill or in a sunny place. Most seeds take two months or longer to sprout, so you must be patient. Take the plastic bags off as soon as the seedlings appear and water the baby trees every week.

Plant the trees outside in autumn. Do not put them too near houses as they will grow long roots. Dig holes a bit bigger than the pots.

Plant each tree in a hole and put a strong cane in next to it. Fill in the soil and press it down, tie the tree to the cane, then water it.

Matching seeds and leaves

You can find out what a tree is by looking at its leaves. Can you match these leaves with the seeds on the opposite page? The answers are at the side of the page.

I PLANTED THIS TREE WHEN I WAS YOUR AGE

Keep a tree sketchbook and draw new trees you see. Or keep a diary about a tree and write down when the leaves and seeds appear.

Answer: 1D,2C,3E,4A,5F,6B.

9

Planting bulbs

Bulbs · Potting soil · Gravel · Pots

CROCUS · DAFFODIL · BLUEBELL · SNOWDROP · TULIP

BULBS ARE EASY TO GROW INDOORS. PLANT THEM IN THE AUTUMN AND THEY WILL FLOWER IN THE WINTER AND SPRING

Most of the first spring flowers grow from bulbs, which are a kind of underground food store. These plants rest for part of the year then use the food in the bulbs to grow in spring. When the leaves die they send food back to the bulb

If you cut a bulb in half you can see the baby plant inside, ready to grow.

Half fill your pots with potting soil. Put the bulbs on top, pointed end up and close together, then fill the pots with more soil. Small bulbs must be covered. Big ones can poke out of the soil. Water them.

10

PUT THE POTS IN A COOL, DARK PLACE FOR 8-10 WEEKS AND THE BULBS WILL START TO GROW. THEY WILL ONLY GROW WHEN IT IS COOL. CHECK THE SOIL NOW AND THEN TO SEE IT IS DAMP

When the buds are about 2in. high, put the pots in a light but cool place. Water the plants regularly.

When they are taller, move them to a warmer place. Push in sticks to support droopy plants. When the flowers die, cut off the heads but leave the leaves. Plant the bulbs outside if you can as they won't flower indoors again.

KEEP THE WATER LEVEL UP

Growing a hyacinth in water

Fill a bulb jar with water to just below the bulb. Put it in a dark place until the roots are 4in. long. A few bits of charcoal in the water help to keep it clean.

11

Window boxes

Window box

Stones

Potting soil

Pitchfork and trowel

Seeds and bulbs

Small plants

YOU CAN PUT POTS ON THE WINDOW LEDGE INSTEAD, AS LONG AS THEY ARE SECURE AND CAN'T FALL OFF

You need a strong, deep window ledge for a window box. A box full of soil is heavy and must be safe. Ask an adult to set yours up for you. It is best if the box tilts back a little, so wedge pieces of wood under the front edge.

Filling the box

POTTING SOIL IS BETTER THAN GARDEN SOIL AS IT CONTAINS ALL THE FOOD YOUR PLANTS NEED TO GROW STRONG AND HEALTHY

Put a layer of gravel or broken pots in the bottom of your box. This stops the soil from getting soggy. Fill the rest of the box with potting soil and rake it to make it level.

Planting

Dig a small hole for each plant. Put it in carefully so the roots have enough room, then press down the soil.

You can grow bulbs, seeds and plants in your window box. Find out when different plants flower, then plan what to plant. Do you know what the flowers in these window boxes are?

Spring

ALWAYS PLANT TALL FLOWERS AT THE BACK OF THE BOX AND SMALL ONES AT THE FRONT

Bulbs flower in spring (see page 10). When they have finished flowering, dig them up, rake the soil and plant seeds for summer flowers.

Summer

You can grow flowers from seed for the summer or put in small plants. The soil in window boxes dries out quickly, so remember to water it often.

Autumn

CUT OFF THE DEAD FLOWER HEADS TO MAKE YOUR PLANTS KEEP FLOWERING

These flowers bloom until the first frosts. Put geraniums in pots and bring them indoors for the winter. Plant spring bulbs early in autumn.

Winter

Winter is the resting time for plants. Cut off dead leaves, pull up weeds and rake over the soil. Then wait for the first spring shoots to appear.

Spring: tulips, forget-me-nots, grape hyacinths.
Summer: marigolds, morning glory, daisies

Autumn: geraniums, lobelia
Winter: snowdrops

13

Growing herbs

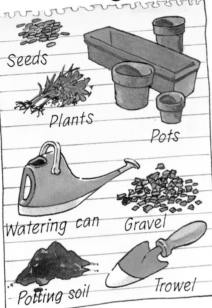

Seeds

Plants

Pots

Watering can

Gravel

Potting soil

Trowel

Cooking

Perfumes

Medicine

People have grown herbs for thousands of years. They have used them to flavor food and to make perfumes and medicines. In the past many people even thought that herbs had magic powers and could keep witches away.

SNIFF SNIFF

An herb's scent comes from oils in its leaves. You smell them if you crush a leaf. Cooks chop herbs to bring out the flavor.

You can buy herbs as plants or grow them from seed (see page 4). You can grow them in the garden, in window boxes or in flowerpots on a sunny windowsill. Herbs need well-drained soil, so if you grow them in pots, remember to put some gravel or broken pot in the bottom.

Parsley

This only lives for one year. It is best to buy plants. It likes some shade and a lot of water.

Thyme

Likes shade. Keep soil damp. Pick leaves as you need them.

Mint

Small shrub. Likes sun. Bees like the flowers.

YOU CAN DRY THYME BY TYING BUNCHES OF IT UPSIDE DOWN IN AN AIRY PLACE FOR TWO WEEKS. WHEN IT IS DRY, RUB THE LEAVES OFF THE STEMS AND PUT THEM IN AN AIRTIGHT JAR

Rosemary

Evergreen shrub. Grows up to 6½ feet tall. Likes a sunny, sheltered place.

Tarragon

DO NOT LET YOUR HERBS FLOWER IF YOU ARE GOING TO USE THEM FOR COOKING. PICK OFF FLOWER BUDS AND THE LEAVES WILL GROW MORE BUSHY

PICK HERBS AS YOU NEED THEM. ALWAYS CUT A GROWING SHOOT AS THIS MAKES THE PLANT GROW STRONG AND BUSHY

Needs a sunny, sheltered place. Grows up to three feet tall.

Chives

Grow in clumps. Pink flowers. Need a lot of water. Have an oniony taste.

Tomatoes

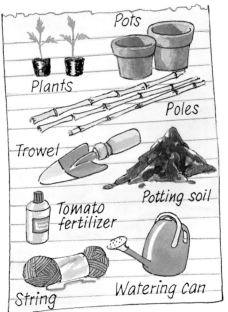

Plants • Pots • Poles • Trowel • Potting soil • Tomato fertilizer • String • Watering can

Tall one-stemmed plant

Small bush plant

Ordinary

Cherry

Beefsteak

Yellow

Plum

Home-grown tomatoes taste much better than the ones you buy in shops. You can grow them from seed (see page 4) or buy small plants, and you can grow them indoors or outdoors, as long as they have a sunny, sheltered spot.

Planting

Fill a big pot, about 10in. across, with potting soil. Put a pole in it and dig a small hole.

Tip the plant out of its pot, keeping all the soil around its roots, and plant it in the big pot.

Fill in more soil around it and press it down firmly. Then give the soil a good watering.

The growing plant

ALWAYS WATER THE ROOTS, NOT THE LEAVES

Put your plant in a warm, sunny place. Water it often to keep the soil damp. Tie the plant loosely to to the pole as it grows taller. When it flowers, shake it gently once a day. This helps to scatter the pollen.

Pinch off side shoots that grow where the leaf stalks join the stem. This makes the plant grow stronger.

Pick the tomatoes when they are ripe and red, with the stalk still on the tomato.

When there are four bunches of tomatoes on the plant, pinch off the top shoot to stop it growing.

17

Growing beans

stones

Large pots

Potting soil

String

seeds

WHEN THE BEANS REACH THE TOP OF THE POLES, PINCH OFF THE TOP GROWING SHOOTS

You don't need a garden to grow vegetables. Here are some you can grow in pots on a balcony or patio.

Fill a bucket-sized pot with potting soil. Stick three poles in it and tie them together at the top to make a climbing frame.

Plant a seed next to each stick and water them. Shoots will appear in 2-3 weeks. As the stems grow, twist them around the poles.

Water the soil often to keep it damp. When flowers appear, spray them with water. This helps the pods to grow.

Pick the beans when they are young. They should be about 4in. long and snap easily when bent.

Potatoes

THE SOIL MUST STAY DAMP, SO DON'T FORGET TO WATER IT

Find a sprouting potato and put it on a warm windowsill until the shoots are 1in. long. Leave two shoots and rub the rest off.

Put stones in the bottom of a 10in. pot and half fill it with potting compost. Plant the potato with the shoots at the top and water it. In about a month green shoots will appear. Add enough compost to cover them. Keep doing this as the shoots grow until the bucket is full.

After a while the plant will flower. Stop watering it when the flowers die, as the baby potatoes will rot if the soil is too wet.

Wait until the whole plant dies, then tip the pot out onto newspaper and see how many potatoes you have grown.

19

Houseplants

Watering can

Potting soil

Spray can

Liquid plant food

Sponge

String

Stakes

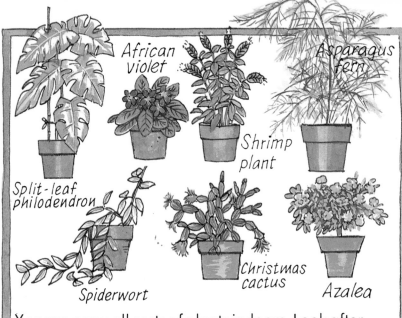

African violet

Asparagus fern

Shrimp plant

Split-leaf philodendron

Spiderwort

Christmas cactus

Azalea

You can grow all sorts of plants indoors. Look after them carefully and watch out for insect pests.

Buying a plant

NEVER OVERWATER A PLANT AS THIS CAN KILL IT

When you buy a plant, read its label or look in a book to see what kind of light and warmth it needs before you decide where to put it. Some plants like light and others shade. None of them like to be in a drafty place.

Water a plant when its soil is dry and more often in hot weather. It is often best to put water in the saucer, not on the plant.

Looking after your plants

Spray plants with water from time to time to clean them. Wipe dusty leaves with a damp cloth and cut off dead leaves and flower heads.

A tall plant needs support to keep it from flopping over. Put a stake in the soil and tie the stems to it loosely as the plant grows.

Plants grow faster in the spring and summer. You can make them grow bushier by picking off the growing tips of the shoots.

You can have an indoor garden in any light room in the house.

I TALK TO MY PLANTS WHEN I'M IN THE BATHTUB

TARZAN

When a plant's roots are too big for its pot, repot it in a larger pot, with new soil. Water it and put it in a shady place for a week.

21

Making baby plants

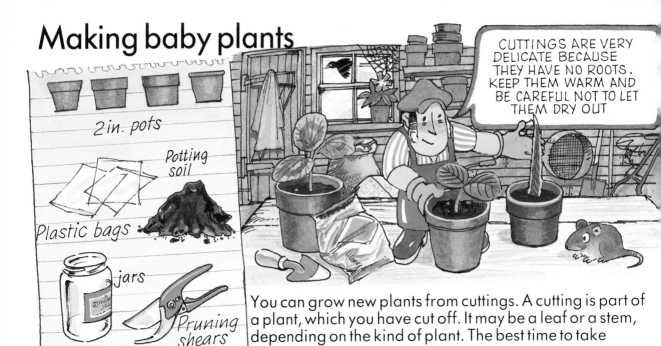

CUTTINGS ARE VERY DELICATE BECAUSE THEY HAVE NO ROOTS. KEEP THEM WARM AND BE CAREFUL NOT TO LET THEM DRY OUT

2 in. pots

Potting soil

Plastic bags

jars

Pruning shears

You can grow new plants from cuttings. A cutting is part of a plant, which you have cut off. It may be a leaf or a stem, depending on the kind of plant. The best time to take cuttings is spring or summer.

Leaf cuttings (African Violet, Begonia, Gloxinia)

Cut a healthy leaf and its stem off a plant. Plant the stem in a pot of cutting soil. Water it, cover it with a jar and put it in a warm, light place.

Baby plants will appear at the bottom of the leaf stem in about six weeks. When they look strong enough you can separate them and plant each one in its own pot.

tem cuttings (Geraniums, Spiderwort)

ut off a strong shoot
bout 4in. long, just
elow a leaf. Trim off the
ottom leaves. Fill a small
ot with cuttings compost.

Gently plant the cutting up
to its leaves. Water it,
cover it with a plastic bag
and put it in a warm place
out of the sun.

After a week or two take
the bag off and pull the
cutting gently. If it feels
firm, it has rooted and you
can leave the bag off.

spider plant grows baby plants with roots at the end of
unners. When the roots are about 1in. long, cut the baby
lants off the runners and plant them in small pots of
ompost, making sure their roots are covered.

Plant presents

Look after your baby
plants and you can give
your friends presents you
have grown yourself.

23

Garden calendar

This calendar is a guide to when to plant the things in this book. The times shown go from the earliest date you can plant something to the latest date. They can change a bit from one year to another, depending on how cold the weather is.

Name	Spring	Summer	Autumn
Flowers			
Trees			
Tomatoes			
Bulbs			
Herbs			
Sun-Flowers			
Beans			
Potatoes			

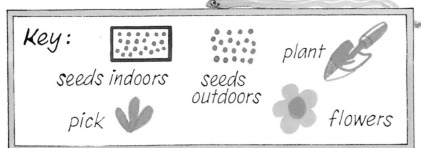

Key:

seeds indoors

seeds outdoors

plant

pick

flowers

READ THE BACKS OF SEED PACKETS TO FIND OUT EXACTLY WHEN TO PLANT DIFFERENT KINDS OF SEEDS

PARTY FUN

Clare Rosen
Illustrated by Lily Whitlock

CONTENTS

Giving A Party

Guests
Matthew
Anna
Freddy
Jane

Games
Treasure hunt
—treasure
10 clues
Peas and straws
—peas
straws
cups

Food
cake
rolls
cookies
ice cream
sausages

SHUT YOUR PETS IN A QUIET ROOM WHILE YOU ARE HAVING THE PARTY

If you plan your party well it will be really good. Send out the invitations about two weeks before the day.

Make a list of friends you want to ask. Count how many there are so you know how much of everything to make.

Then make a list of the games you are going to play and the things you will need for each game.

Get as many things ready as you can the day before the party. Make the cake and put it in an airtight can.

Before the party starts put a bunch of balloons on your door or gate so that your guests can find the house easily.

Themes

There are lots of different types of parties. If you choose a theme, make your invitation fit the theme (see page 28), and tell your guests what to wear. If the weather is fine, you could have an outdoor party, like a picnic or a barbecue, but you will need help from an adult.

Monster party

Make a monster pop-up invitation and tell your guests to look ugly! Make monster masks and brightly colored food.

Color party

Ask your guests to dress in one color, for example, yellow. Then make yellow streamers and lanterns. Dye the food with yellow food dye and make banana milk shakes.

Disco party

Put colored light bulbs in the lights and hold a disco dancing competition.

Zoo or Farm party

Draw animal faces on balloons. Make animal invitations and place names. Make a cucumber crocodile (see page 35).

Spooky party

Make ghost invitations and spooky decorations.

Pop-up Invitations

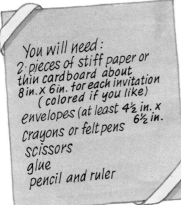

You will need :
2 pieces of stiff paper or thin cardboard about 8 in. x 6 in. for each invitation (colored if you like)
envelopes (at least 4½ in. x 6½ in.)
crayons or felt pens
scissors
glue
pencil and ruler

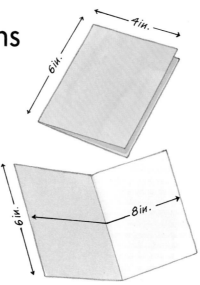

The picture inside the invitation pops up when the card is opened.

Fold two pieces of paper in half, crossways, as shown. One piece is for the card, the other for the pop-up.

To make the pop-up, fold one piece of paper in half again. Open it out, then cut out one quarter. Fold it in half crossways.

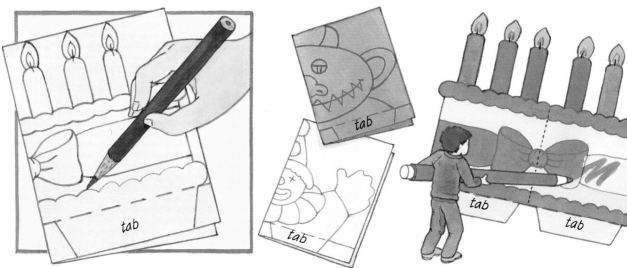

Draw half a cake against the fold. (You could draw any party thing like a clown or some balloons. Make it fit your party theme if you have one.) Leave a small space at the bottom of the paper and draw a tab on the bottom edge.

Cut out the picture and open it out. You will have a cut-out of a whole cake with two tabs on it. Color it in.

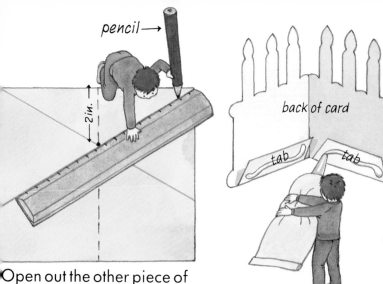

pencil →

2 in.

Open out the other piece of paper. Measure 2in. along the fold and make a dot. Draw lines across the card from the top corners through the dot to the other sides.

back of card

tab   tab

Fold the tabs on the cake back along the dotted lines, and put a little glue on the bottom of each one.

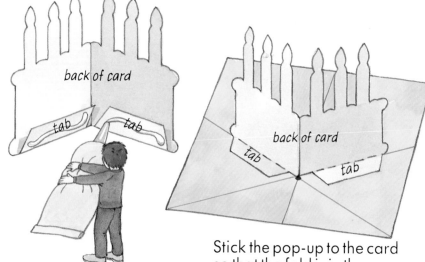

back of card

tab   tab

Stick the pop-up to the card so that the fold is in the middle of the card and the sides are along two of the lines, as shown. Press the tabs down.

On May 16th.
From 4-6pm
At 4 Hanover Place
Toledo
tel: 691 0030
RSVP

Sam would like Jane to come to his birthday party

Come as   a Monster

Leave the glue to dry, then erase the pencil lines. Fold the card and draw a picture on the front.

On the inside of the card write the name of the guest, and when and where you are having your party. Write RSVP in the bottom corner. This means "Please reply."

Decorations

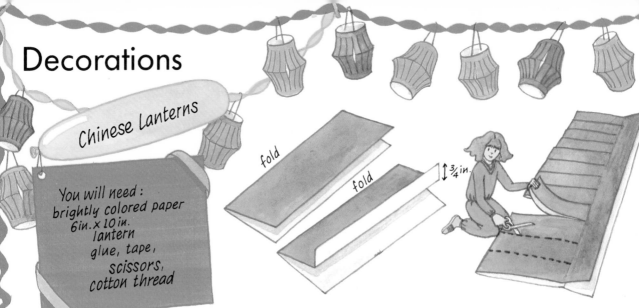

You will need:
brightly colored paper
6 in. x 10 in.
lantern
glue, tape,
scissors,
cotton thread

fold

fold

¾ in.

You can make a garland of lanterns by hanging some of them from a streamer.

Fold the paper in half lengthwise. Make folds ¾in. in along the long edges of the paper, as shown.

Open out the ¾in. folds. Cut strips about ¾in. wide where the dotted lines are in the picture, as far as the fold.

Streamers

You will need:
at least one packet of crepe paper
tape
scissors

crepe

Cut it into strips 2in. wide.

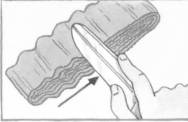

Run the scissors down both edges of the strips to curl them.

Unwind the strips and join them together with tape. Twist the streamers and stick them to the ceiling.

Keep the paper folded as it is in the packet.

Open out the paper. Spread glue all along one of the end strips.

Bend the paper into a tube and stick the two end strips together. Stick a long piece of thread to both sides of the top edge with tape so you can hang up your lantern.

Decorated Balloons

You will need:
a packet of balloons
brightly colored paper
glue, scissors
felt pens, straws
string

Have enough balloons to give one to each of your guests when they leave.

Blow up the balloons. Cut out shapes, pictures or faces from the colored paper that fit the theme of your party.

Put a dab of glue onto each shape; then stick them onto the balloons. Tie a long piece of string to each one.

31

Masks

You will need:
thin cardboard
paper
very thin elastic

things for decoration,
such as:
paints, glitter,
feathers, straws,
pipe cleaners,
silver paper,
plastic cups,
etc.

Masks are always fun at a party. Make one for each of your friends. They will have to guess who the other guests are. Make spooky masks for a Halloween party, ugly ones for a monster party and animal ones for a zoo party.

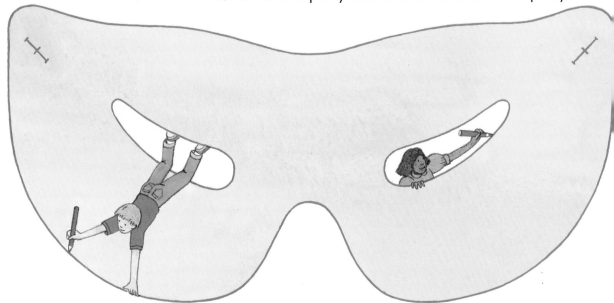

Use this pattern to make your masks. Trace it onto paper, then cut out the tracing.

Lay the tracing on a piece of cardboard and draw around it. Then cut it out carefully.

32

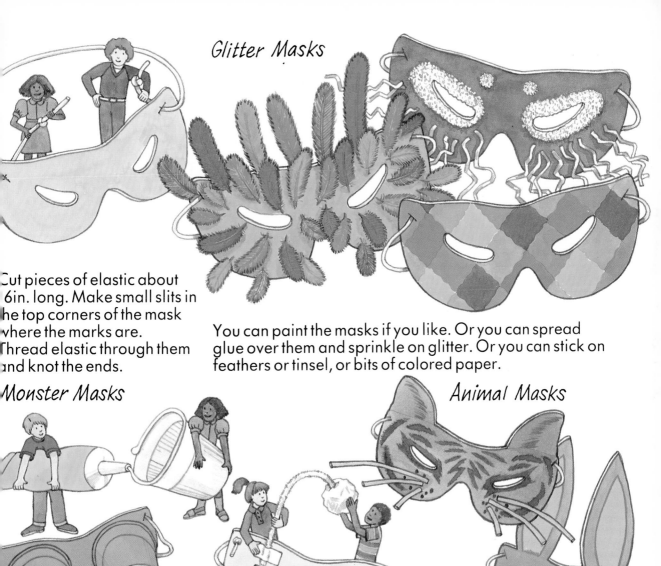

Glitter Masks

Cut pieces of elastic about 16in. long. Make small slits in the top corners of the mask where the marks are. Thread elastic through them and knot the ends.

You can paint the masks if you like. Or you can spread glue over them and sprinkle on glitter. Or you can stick on feathers or tinsel, or bits of colored paper.

Monster Masks

Cut holes in the bottoms of paper cups and glue them over the eye holes. You can make "feelers" by sticking pipe cleaners onto the backs of the masks with tape. Bend the ends over and crumple silver paper around them in balls.

Animal Masks

Paint the masks to look like animals. To make whiskers, glue straws on either side. Stick on paper ears.

Place Cards

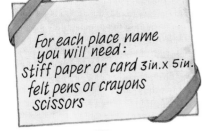

For each place name you will need:
stiff paper or card 3 in. x 5 in.
felt pens or crayons
scissors

Joe

Make place cards for all your guests to show them where to sit.

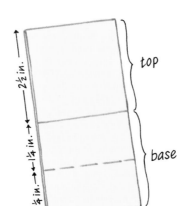

top

base

2½ in.

1¼ in.

1¼ in.

Fold the card in half. Fold one of the halves in half again. Open out the card.

Draw a simple picture on the top half of the card. Make it fit your party theme if you have one.

Kate

Tessa

Tom

Richard

Sarah

Jenny

Color in the picture with felt pens or crayons, then cut around it.

Bend the base back in half along the fold. Write the name of one of your guests on the base and stand the card on their plate.

Party Food

MAKE DELICIOUS LEMONADE OR COCOA FOR YOUR FRIENDS. MAKE SURE THERE IS ENOUGH FOOD FOR EVERYONE AND THAT IT LOOKS GOOD

sausages

chips

cookies

cheese crackers

hard boiled eggs

candy

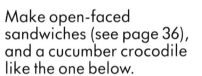
toast fingers

carrot and celery sticks

grapes

Make open-faced sandwiches (see page 36), and a cucumber crocodile like the one below.

Fill bowls with chips and bite-sized things that people can eat with their fingers. Finish the treat with ice cream sundaes (see page 37) and a special cake (see page 38).

Cucumber Crocodile

You will need: a cucumber, small can of pineapple chunks, about 8 oz. cheddar cheese, two stuffed olives, 2 carrots, toothpicks

Make a slit in the fat end of the cucumber for a mouth. Make its eyes out of olives stuck onto toothpicks.

Make two holes at each end of the cucumber and stick short pieces of carrot in them for legs. Put cubes

of cheese and chunks of pineapple on toothpicks and stick them all along the crocodile like scales.

Snacks

Make delicious snacks with all sorts of different toppings, like these.

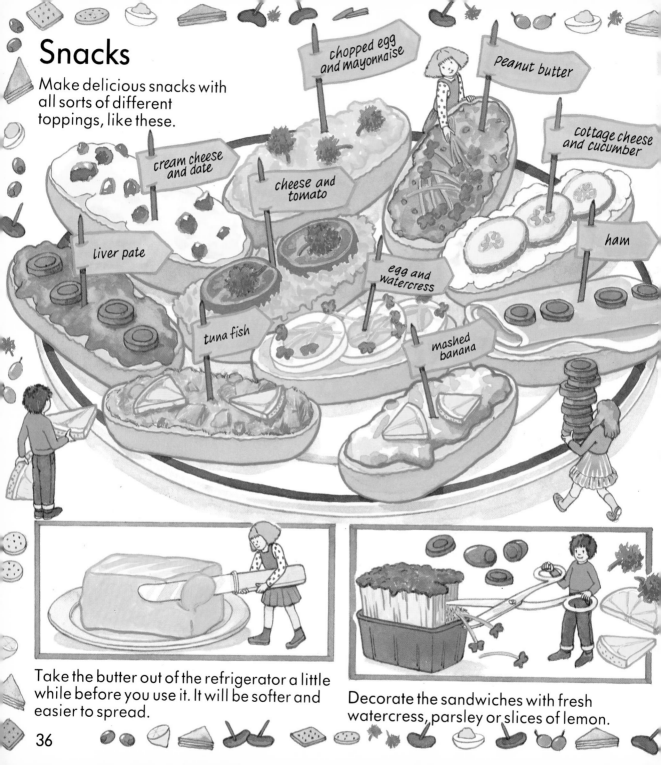

chopped egg and mayonnaise

peanut butter

cream cheese and date

cheese and tomato

cottage cheese and cucumber

liver pate

ham

egg and watercress

tuna fish

mashed banana

Take the butter out of the refrigerator a little while before you use it. It will be softer and easier to spread.

Decorate the sandwiches with fresh watercress, parsley or slices of lemon.

Ice Cream Sundaes

You will need:
ice cream, fresh fruit, canned peach halves plain chocolate, wafers, chopped nuts, candied cherries for decoration

Ice cream sundaes are made with ice cream, fruit, and sometimes sauce. Add a dollop of whipped cream if you like. Make them just before your party and keep them in the refrigerator.

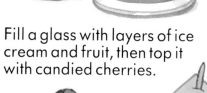

skyscraper

peach boat

Fill a glass with layers of ice cream and fruit, then top it with candied cherries.

Put half a canned peach on a plate. Fill it with a scoop of ice cream and stick a wafer in it for a sail.

chocolate sauce

Break 4oz. plain chocolate into the top of a double boiler with 3 tablespoons water. Heat it over hot water until it melts.

banana split

Put two scoops of ice cream on a plate. Cut a banana in half lengthways and stick the halves to either side of the ice cream. Decorate it with chopped nuts and grated chocolate, or pour chocolate sauce over it.

Party Chocolate Cake

THE BOWL GETS VERY HOT. USE OVEN MITTS TO LIFT IT

You will need:
6 oz. unsweetened chocolate
6 teaspoons water
6 oz. butter or margarine
6 oz. soft dark brown sugar
4 large eggs
3 oz. ground almonds
3 oz. white bread crumbs
apricot jam

Grease two 9in. cake pans. Set the oven to 375°F.

Melt the chocolate with the water in the top of a double boiler over hot water until it melts. Stir well.

Beat the butter in a bowl until it is soft, then beat in the sugar until it is fluffy.

Separate the egg whites from the yolks. You need two bowls. Crack each egg over one of the bowls, then slip the yolk from one half of the shell to the other. The white will slip into the bowl below. Put the yolk in the second bowl.

Beat the egg yolks, ground almonds, melted chocolate and grated bread crumbs into the butter mixture.

Whisk the egg whites until they stand up in peaks. Fold them into the chocolate mixture with a metal spoon.

Spread half the mixture into each cake pan. Bake for about 20 minutes, until the centers feel springy.

When the cakes are cool, slip a knife around the sides of the pans and turn them out. Stick the two cakes together with apricot jam.

Icing

You will need:

3 tablespoons Corn Syrup
3 oz. butter
3 tablespoons cocoa powder

Melt the syrup with the butter over a low heat, then beat in the cocoa powder with a fork.

Beat the icing until thick, then pour it over the cake. Smooth it all around the cake with a knife.

Decorate the cake before the icing sets. If you are having candles put them firmly in holders.

Drinks

Fruity Milk Shakes

For eight guests
you will need:

3 pints milk
1lb. soft fruit
(e.g. bananas, strawberries)
or 10 oz.
can of fruit
(e.g. apricots,
pineapple)
3 table-
spoons
sugar

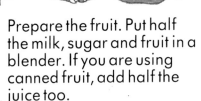

PEEL THE FRUIT AND
TAKE OUT ANY PITS
OR STEMS

Prepare the fruit. Put half the milk, sugar and fruit in a blender. If you are using canned fruit, add half the juice too.

Put the lid on firmly and blend for 30 seconds. Pour it into glasses. Blend the other half of the ingredients.

If you do not have a blender, mash the fruit with a fork, then whisk it into the milk.

Pour the milk shakes into tall glasses. Put straws in them. You can decorate the drinks with sprigs of mint or you could grate chocolate on top.

Fizzy Fruit Punch

For eight guests you will need:

1 quart carton unsweetened fresh orange juice
1 quart lemonade
an apple, orange and lemon
ice cubes
some sprigs of mint

You should make fizzy fruit punch just before your party so the lemonade is still fizzy.

Wash the apple, cut it into quarters and cut out the core. Chop it up. Slice the orange and lemon.

Put the fruit into a large jug or bowl. Add the ice cubes and mint.

Pour the orange juice over the fruit, ice and mint. Then add the lemonade and stir everything gently together.

Indoor Games

Peas and Straws

For each player you will need:
a straw
2 cups
30 dried peas

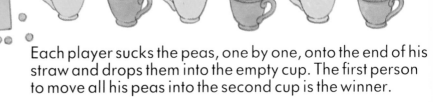

Each player is given two cups. One is empty and the other has 30 peas in it.

Each player sucks the peas, one by one, onto the end of his straw and drops them into the empty cup. The first person to move all his peas into the second cup is the winner.

Eaties

For each player you will need:
a blindfold
a plate
10 different kinds of food (include things like dry cereal and spaghetti)

Put a bit of each kind of food on every plate.

Blindfold the players and give them all a plate of food. When they have eaten everything, take the plates away. Take off the blindfolds, so they can write down what they ate. The person to get most things right is the winner.

The Tray Game

You will need:
a large tray
about 20 small objects
pencils and paper

Put the things on the tray. Give your guests 3 minutes to look at it, then take it away.

The players must try to write down everything that was on the tray. The one who remembers the most things is the win

42

Treasure Hunt

You will need:
10 small pieces of paper and a pencil
treasure (a small present or some wrapped candies)

First hide the treasure somewhere difficult to find.

Then write the clues on bits of paper. Each clue tells the players where to find the next clue. Hide the clues around the house. The last clue says where the treasure is.

Read out the first clue to everyone. Ask the players to put the clues back after they have read them. In this hunt, the first clue is—

1. I keep you dry — look in me for the next clue.

4. Monkeys love me — look under me for the next clue.

6. The next clue will come splashing out if you turn me on.

7. You dream on me — look under me to find the treasure.

2. I am soft and blue — look under me for the next clue.

5. You pick me up to stop me ringing — and find the next clue.

3. I light your bed-time story — look under me for the next clue.

Treasure is hidden under the bed.

43

Outdoor Games

Flowerpot Race

You will need:
- 4 plastic flowerpots
- 4 pieces of string at least twice as long as your legs
- scissors

10 yards

To make the stilts, make a hole on each side of the flower pots with the point of the scissors, near the base. Pull a piece of string through the holes and knot the ends tightly.

The players stand in two teams. Put a marker about 10 yards from each team.

The first player in each team stands on the flower pot stilts, holds the string, walks to the marker, around it and back. He gives the stilts to the next player. The first team to all get around the marker and back wins.

Chocolate medals

You can give chocolate medals to the team who wins (see page 46).

Mailbox Game

You will need:
8 boxes, jars or cans
paper and a pen
tape
a table

Mailboxes

Rome
Paris
Athens
London
Tokyo
Bonn
Moscow
Lisbon

Letters

In this game the players must mail their letters in the right boxes – the Rome letter goes in the Rome box.

Write the name of eight capital cities on pieces of paper. Stick them to the eight boxes, jars or cans with tape. Hide the mailboxes around the yard.

To make letters, cut out eight small pieces of paper for each guest. There is one letter for each mailbox.

Write the name of one of the cities on each letter. Make a pile of letters for each player on a table.

Each player takes one letter at a time and writes his name on the back. Then he finds the right box to mail it in. When he has mailed it, he runs back for another letter. Check the boxes. The first player to mail all his letters is the winner.

Chocolate Medals

You will need:

chocolate (about ½ oz. for each medal)
small cupcake liners
a baking sheet, aluminium foil
paper ribbon (the kind you wrap presents with)

Give a chocolate medal to anyone who wins a game.

Melt chocolate in top of a double boiler over hot water.

Put the cupcake liners onto a baking sheet.

Pour melted chocolate into each liner, just covering the bottom. Leave the chocolate to cool and set.

Gently push the chocolate discs out with your thumbs and wrap each one in a piece of aluminium foil.

Cut a piece of paper ribbon about a yard long for each medal.

Stick a ribbon to the back of each medal with tape.

Presents

GIVE YOUR GUESTS A SMALL PRESENT AS THEY LEAVE. WRAP A LITTLE TOY OR GAME IN COLORED TISSUE PAPER OR WRAPPING PAPER.

Present Tree

In the summer you could hang the presents on a small tree or bush.

Tie a piece of yarn or string around each present and hang them from the tree.

Surprise Box

You will need:
a large cardboard box
crepe paper
a newspaper
small, wrapped presents

Cover a cardboard box with crepe paper. Fill the box with a jumble of presents and crumpled newspaper.

When the guests are leaving they can each dip their hand in and find a present.

Going Home Bag

You will need:
colored paper
string
tape
little presents
scissors
felt pens
old magazines

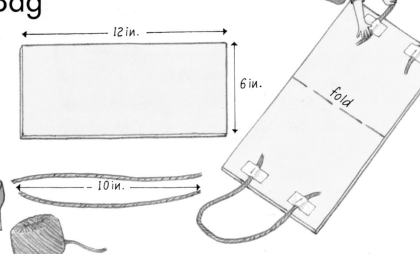

Make little bags for your friends to take home and fill them with tiny surprise presents.

Cut out a strip of paper 12in. by 6in. Cut two 10in. pieces of string.

Stick each piece of string in a loop at either end of the paper like this, to make handles.

Fold the paper in half. Stick the sides together with tape. Write the guest's name on it with felt pens.

Decorate the bag with felt pens or cut pictures out of magazines and stick them on. Make them fit your party theme if you have one.

Put a present in each bag, such as a pencil sharpener or a little notebook, with a balloon and some candy.

DON'T FORGET TO SAY "THANK YOU" WHEN YOU LEAVE A PARTY

MAKING PRESENTS

Clare Rosen
Illustrated by Lily Whitlock

CONTENTS

Hobby Horse

You will need:

a large old sock
scraps of material or newspaper for stuffing
a piece of felt
2 buttons
some yarn
needle and thread
a ribbon
a broom handle

Stuff the foot of the sock firmly with scraps of material or newspaper.

ear

fold line

Trace this shape onto some paper and cut it out. For each ear, pin the shape onto felt and cut around it.

Fold the ears down the middle. Pin them to the sock and sew them on, using backstitch (see page 73).

Sew on buttons for eyes. Sew a mouth in backstitch. Sew a line of yarn loops down the neck for a mane.

Push the broom handle into the sock as far as the heel. Pack stuffing around it. Tie a ribbon around it to hold it on

Pasta Necklace

You will need:
pasta shapes
poster paints
1 yard of ribbon
varnish (clear nail polish will do)

Choose pasta shapes with a hole in the middle so that you can thread them. Paint them bright colors, using thick poster paint.

When the pasta shapes are dry, paint them with a coat of varnish. Wait for them to dry. Thread the shapes onto a ribbon and tie it in a bow.

To make beads hang down, thread the ribbon through two shapes, then back through the first.

Calendar Pictures

You will need:
a piece of
          heavy paper
glue & tape
paints or things to
make a collage with
a calendar booklet
a piece of string

A calendar is easy to make and a good present for anyone at the beginning of the year. You could paint a picture or make a collage out of scraps of paper or odds and ends.

You can make a collage out of beans, rice, lentils or pasta. First draw a picture on a piece of heavy paper.

You will need:
a piece of heavy paper
flowers and/or leaves
blotting paper
large books
glue and tape
a calendar booklet
a piece of string

To make a picture from pressed flowers and leaves, you must collect them a few weeks in advance.

Carefully lay the flowers and leaves you have picked onto a sheet of blotting paper. Put another piece of blotting paper over them and put them inside a large book.

Spread glue onto part of the picture and press one sort of bean onto it. Glue different beans to each part of the picture.

When the glue is dry, gently shake off any loose bits. Tape a short string to the back, like this.

Glue a calendar booklet onto the bottom of the picture.

DECEMBER

BE CAREFUL WITH YOUR PRESSED FLOWERS—THEY ARE VERY FRAGILE

Close the book and stack heavy books on top. Leave them for at least two weeks.

Arrange the flowers and leaves on the heavy paper, then stick them on using only a tiny spot of glue.

JULY

Candies

Truffles

For about 20 truffles you will need :

⅓ cup cream cheese
1 teaspoon milk
½ cup powdered sugar
½ cup cocoa powder
chocolate sprinkles
cocoa powder for decoration

Mix together the cheese and milk. Stir in the powdered sugar and cocoa. Roll the mixture

into marble-sized balls in cocoa or chocolate sprinkles. Put them in the refrigerator for an hour.

Making Marzipan

½ cup ground almonds
⅓ cup powdered sugar
⅓ cup granulated sugar
1 egg white*
1 teaspoon lemon juice
walnut halves and blanched almonds
dates
red and green food coloring

Mix together the powdered sugar, ground almonds, granulated sugar and lemon. Add enough egg to make a stiff paste.

Divide the mixture into three balls. Add a drop of food coloring to two of the balls and knead it in.

54   *You can buy dried egg white, if you don't want to use uncooked egg white.

Marzinuts

Window Cookies

Roll some of each color marzipan into small balls. Press a nut onto the top of each ball.

Cut four pieces of marzipan, at least one from each color, and roll them into long sausages. Push the rolls firmly together, two on top of the other two, and flatten them on all sides. Slice them into small squares.

Stuffed Dates

Cut open the dates and take out the pits. Fill them with marzipan. Then sprinkle them with sugar.

Put your cookies and candies in a box or basket lined with pretty paper. Or use an empty jar.

55

Humpty Dumpty Egg Warmer

You will need:
pink, yellow, blue and green felt
red & yellow yarn
a large needle
pins
scissors
a felt pen
a ruler
fabric glue

3in

fold line

3 in

fold

1½ in

Cut out a square of paper, each side 3in. long (see p.73). Fold it in half. Measure 1½in. from the top.

corner. Draw a curved line across the corner, where the dotted line is. Cut along the line. Open the paper out.

lining

hands

eyes

fold

legs

nose

3 in

½ i

collar

Fold the yellow felt in half and pin the paper to it. Cut around it. Do the same with the pink felt.

Draw these shapes on different colored pieces of felt, using a felt pen, and cut them out. To make the collar, cut out a piece of felt 3in. by 1in. Fold it in half and cut out a shape for the bow tie, like this.

Glue the collar, eyes and nose onto one piece of yellow felt. Sew a mouth with yarn, using backstitch. *

Turn the felt over. Glue the hands and legs onto the back, as shown. Glue on strips of red yarn for hair.

Glue a pink felt shape onto the back of the yellow piece. Glue the other yellow piece to the other pink one.

Put the two halves together with the pink felt on the inside. Sew them together around the curved edge using blanket stitch. *

Make an egg warmer in a different color for each person.

* See page 73

Kaleidoscope

You will need:

a 6in. square of silver adhesive mylar *
1 sheet of wrapping paper
tracing paper
felt pens
tape and glue
a pencil
scissors and a ruler

*You can buy silver adhesive mylar in art supply shops.

On the plain side of the mylar, measure 2in. along one edge and make a pencil mark. Measure another 2in. along the edge and make another mark. Do the same on the opposite edge and draw between the marks, like this.

Score along the lines using a ruler and the tip of the scissors, like this. Do not cut through the mylar.

Fold the mylar along the lines, so the mirror is inside. Stick the edges together with tape.

Stand the tube on the tracing paper and trace around the end. Do the same on the wrapping paper. Cut out the triangles of paper.

58

Carefully stick the triangle of tracing paper over one end of the tube with tape.

Color the pieces of tracing paper with felt pens. Cut them into little pieces and drop them into the tube.

Stick the wrapping paper triangle over the open end of the tube and make a hole in the middle with a pencil.

Cut out a piece of wrapping paper 6¾in. long and 6in. wide. Lay the tube down on it a little way from the edge. Glue the paper neatly all around the tube to cover it.

Hold the tube up to the light and look through the hole. Shake the kaleidoscope to make the patterns change.

59

Poppies and Daffodils

crepe paper
10in lengths of garden
wire for stems
black paper
strong glue
with a spout
scissors

poppies

Flower Center

Cut out a piece of black paper about this size. Make cuts all along it, as shown.

Spread glue along it and wind it around the end of a wire stem.

Petals

grain

Cut eight petals like this out of crepe paper. Cut them so the grain (the crinkles) are running up and down.

Shape the petals by stretching them a bit with your thumbs, like this. Then glue them around the center.

Glue a long strip of green crepe paper to the bottom of the flower. Wind it down the wire and glue the end down.

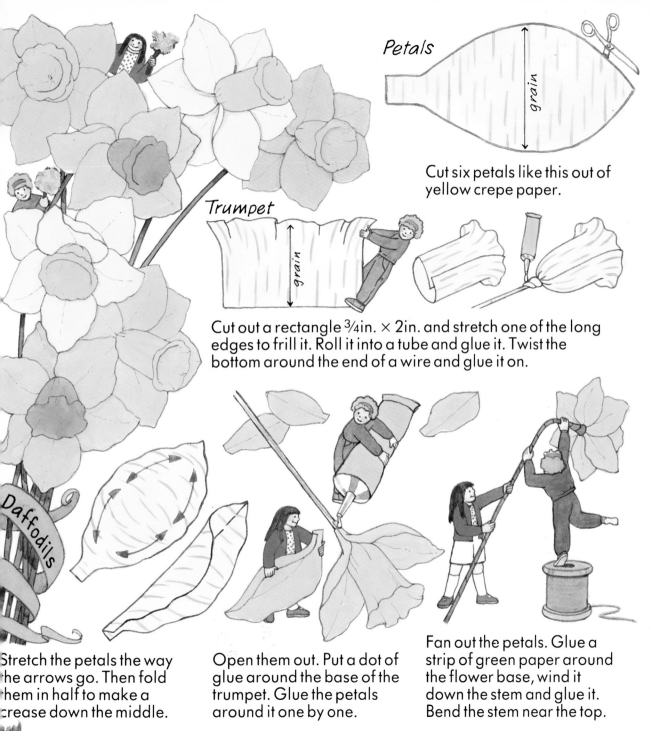

Petals

Cut six petals like this out of yellow crepe paper.

Trumpet

Cut out a rectangle ¾in. × 2in. and stretch one of the long edges to frill it. Roll it into a tube and glue it. Twist the bottom around the end of a wire and glue it on.

Daffodils

Stretch the petals the way the arrows go. Then fold them in half to make a crease down the middle.

Open them out. Put a dot of glue around the base of the trumpet. Glue the petals around it one by one.

Fan out the petals. Glue a strip of green paper around the flower base, wind it down the stem and glue it. Bend the stem near the top.

Painted Eggs

You will need:

eggs
paint & brushes
a big sewing needle
varnish (clear nail
polish will do)

MAKE SURE YOU BREAK THE YOLK

Make a hole in the small end of each egg with a big needle. Make a bigger hole in the other end of the egg.

Blow hard into the small hole until all the egg comes out. Catch it in a bowl and keep it for cooking.

Wash the egg and dry it carefully.

Sit an egg in an egg cup and paint it. Paint one end, leave it to dry and then paint the other end.

If you are using more than one color, paint the lighter colors first. Try different patterns and pictures.

When the egg is completely dry paint it with varnish.

62

Egg Mobile

You will need:

4 painted eggs
3 house plant stakes
cotton thread
string and scissors

Lay two stakes across each other and tie them together in the middle. Leave one end of the string long.

Break four short pieces off the third stake. Tie a long piece of thread to each one.

Push a piece of stake right into the bigger hole of each egg, holding the thread.

ONCE INSIDE, THE STAKE CANNOT GET OUT

Tie the eggs onto the stakes like this, and cut off any long extra thread.

Ask a friend to hold the string for you. Move the eggs along the stakes until the mobile balances well.

Party Hats

Sun Bonnet 21½ in. square of heavy paper crepe paper tissue paper pencil, string, scissors and sticky tape

Wizard's Hat
20 in. square of black or dark blue heavy paper aluminium foil scissors glue and tape

Indian Headdress
corrugated cardboard 20 in long & 2 in wide tissue paper straws scissors, glue and tape paints or felt pens

Wizard's Hat

Cut out a piece of heavy paper 20 in. square.* Fold it into a cone and tape it down.

Trim the bottom edge with scissors to make it straight.

Cut star and moon shapes out of aluminium foil and glue them on to the hat.

Sun Bonnet

Cut a circle with a 10in. radius out of heavy paper.★ Cut two slits opposite each other, 3in. from the center.

Cut the ribbon of crepe paper about 4in. wide and 1 yard long. Fold it in half lengthways and thread it through the slits. Make some paper flowers (see page 12) and stick them onto the hat with tape.

Indian Headdress

Cut out a piece of corrugated cardboard 20in. long and 2in. wide.

Paint a pattern on it. When the paint is dry, stick the ends together with tape.

Cut feather shapes out of tissue paper. Make them a little shorter than the straws.

Glue the feathers onto the straws. Leave about 2in. of straw at the bottom.

Make cuts along the feathers, as shown.

Push the ends of the straws into the holes in the cardboard.

★ See page 73

Desk Organizer

Penholder

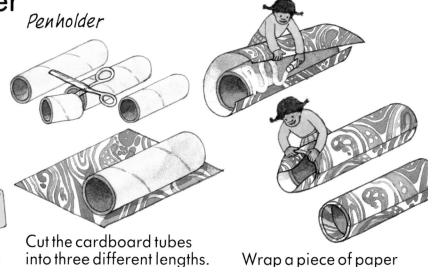

You will need:
3 cardboard tubes (from kitchen or bathroom paper rolls)
2 sheets of wrapping paper
a piece of heavy paper about 8in. x 6in.
4 empty matchboxes
scissors and glue
4 paper fasteners

This is a good present for a grown-up. It holds all sorts of useful things like pens, pencils and stamps.

Cut the cardboard tubes into three different lengths. Cut out pieces of paper big enough to go around each, with a little left over.

Wrap a piece of paper around each tube. Glue the edges together and fold in the overlap at each end.

Base

Stamp Box

NEVER PLAY WITH MATCHES

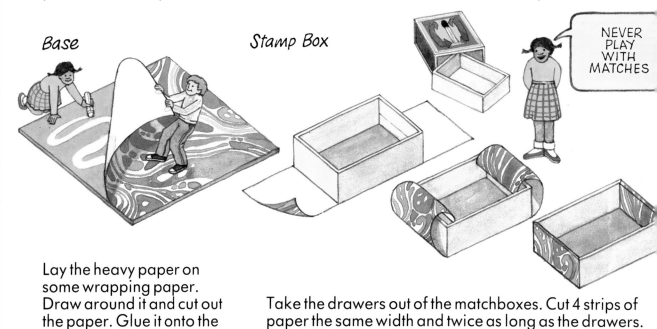

Lay the heavy paper on some wrapping paper. Draw around it and cut out the paper. Glue it onto the heavy paper to make the base.

Take the drawers out of the matchboxes. Cut 4 strips of paper the same width and twice as long as the drawers. Wrap them around the drawers and glue them on.

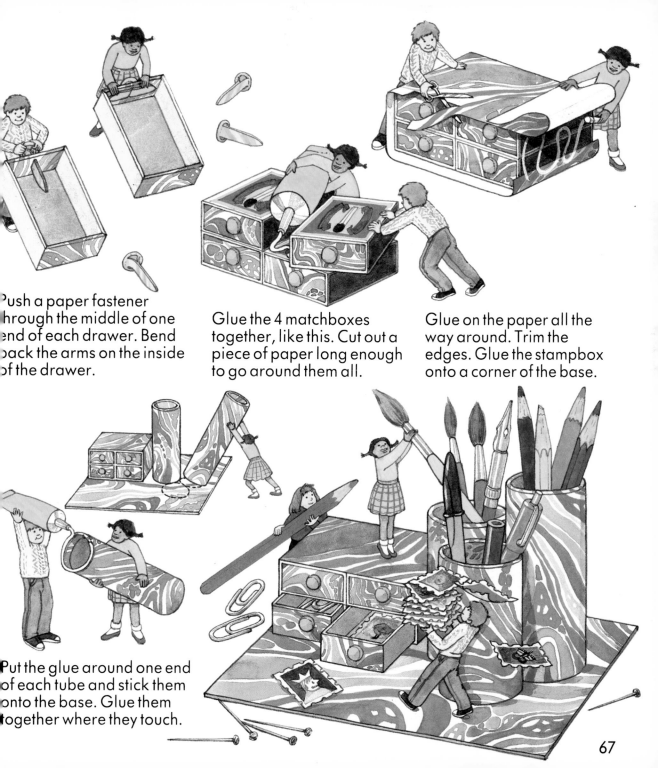

Push a paper fastener through the middle of one end of each drawer. Bend back the arms on the inside of the drawer.

Glue the 4 matchboxes together, like this. Cut out a piece of paper long enough to go around them all.

Glue on the paper all the way around. Trim the edges. Glue the stampbox onto a corner of the base.

Put the glue around one end of each tube and stick them onto the base. Glue them together where they touch.

Piggy Bank

You will need:

four pages of newspaper
paste and strong glue
    with a spout
an orange
four toothpaste tops
a cork
poster paint
varnish (clear nail
        polish will do)

You can make this pig out of "papier-mâché," which means mashed paper. It takes some time to make.

Tear the newspaper into small pieces. Put them in a bowl of water to soak for a few minutes.

Press a layer of paper arour the orange. Put paste all ove it, then another layer of paper. Do this until there are six layers of paper.

Put the orange somewhere warm overnight. When the paper is dry cut it around the orange. Take out the orange. Cut a slot as big as a large coin along the edge of one half. Glue the halves back together again.

Cover the ball with two more layers of paper. Use the newspaper margins so the ball ends up white.

Glue four toothpaste tube tops onto the bottom for legs. Cut the end off a cork with a knife and glue it on for a nose.

Put another layer of glue and paper all over the piggy, covering the legs and nose.

Paint the pig with thick paint. When it is dry, paint on a face and a tail.

When the paint is dry, you can varnish it to make it shiny.

Printing Paper

Marbling

You will need:

FOR MARBLING
2 colors of oil paint *
turpentine
a big bowl, a plate
& a knife

FOR POTATO PRINTS
a big potato
a knife and a plate
paints
paper

FOR STENCILS
index card
paints and scissors
an old toothbrush
paper

ALWAYS PUT THE
TOP BACK ON THE
TURPENTINE BOTTLE
RIGHT AWAY

Put blobs of the paint on a plate. Mix a few drops of turpentine into it with a knife to make it runny.

Pour a little water into a bowl. The bowl must be at least as big as your paper.

Shake the paint from the knife onto the water and swirl it around.

Gently lay your paper on top of the water, then carefully lift it off again. Leave the paper to dry.

Clean the plate, knife and bowl with turpentine, then wash them in hot soapy wat

*You can buy small tubes of oil paint at art shops.

Potato Prints

DON'T FORGET THAT YOUR PRINT WILL COME OUT BACKWARDS

Cut a big potato in half. Cut a shape on the flat side, then cut away the potato around it so the shape stands out.

Mix some paint with a little water on a plate. Press the cut side of the potato down into it.

Press the potato onto paper to make a print of the shape. Make more prints all over the paper to make a pattern.

Stencils

Draw a shape on a piece of index card. Push the point of your scissors into it and cut it out to make a stencil.

Hold the stencil down firmly on a big piece of paper. Dip an old toothbrush into paint. Hold it over the stencil and stroke the bristles.

Spatter the paint evenly over the stencil shape. Lift off the stencil and do the same again until the pattern is all over the paper.

Wrapping Presents

You will need:
wrapping
paper
tape
ribbon

MAKE YOUR
PRESENTS LOOK A
PRETTY AS POSSIBI
WRAP COLORED
RIBBON OR TAPE
ROUND THEM
AND TIE ON
BOWS

Square present

IF THE PRESENT IS
BREAKABLE OR A DIFFICULT
SHAPE TO WRAP, PUT IT
IN A BOX FIRST

Cut out a piece of wrapping paper big
enough to go right around the present.
Wrap it around the present and tape it.

Fold down one end, then fold in the sides.
Fold the bottom flap up and tape it down.
Do the same at the other end.

Round present

Lay the present on the paper.
Cut out the paper so it has a
4in. overlap at each end.

Roll the paper around the present and tape it down in the
middle. Bunch up the ends and twist them a little.